For Missy and Jeff, with love. —L. H. H.

STERLING CHILDREN'S BOOKS
New York

An Imprint of Sterling Publishing
387 Park Avenue South
New York, NY 10016

Text © 2015 by Lori Haskins Houran
Illustrations © 2015 by Sam Usher

The artwork for this book was created using ink and watercolor.
Art direction and design by Merideth Harte.

ISBN 978-1-4549-1062-6

Library of Congress Cataloging-in-Publication Data

Houran, Lori Haskins.
  A dozen cousins / by Lori Houran ; illustrated by Sam Usher.
    pages cm
  Summary: Although her younger cousins--all boys--like to play tricks
on her, nine-year-old Anna takes it all in stride.
  ISBN 978-1-4549-1062-6
  [1. Stories in rhyme. 2. Cousins--Fiction.] I. Usher, Sam, illustrator. II. Title.
  PZ8.3.H789Do 2014
  [E]--dc23

                    2013047276

Distributed in Canada by Sterling Publishing
c/o Canadian Manda Group, 165 Dufferin Street
Toronto, Ontario, Canada M6K 3H6
Distributed in the United Kingdom by GMC Distribution Services
Castle Place, 166 High Street, Lewes, East Sussex, England BN7 1XU
Distributed in Australia by Capricorn Link (Australia) Pty. Ltd.
P.O. Box 704, Windsor, NSW 2756, Australia

For information about custom editions, special sales, and premium and
corporate purchases, please contact Sterling Special Sales at 800-805-5489
or specialsales@sterlingpublishing.com.

Manufactured in China
Lot #:
2 4 6 8 10 9 7 5 3 1
11/14

www.sterlingpublishing.com/kids

A Dozen Cousins

by **LORI HASKINS HOURAN**   illustrated by **SAM USHER**

STERLING CHILDREN'S BOOKS
New York

Anna had a dozen cousins.
All of them were boys.

They smelled like sweaty sneakers,
and they made a ton of noise.

They read her secret diary.

They used up all her paint.

They put a lizard in her hat . . .

to see if she would faint.

Her skirt became a teepee,
her bear, a wrecking ball.

They launched a rocket into space.
The astronaut? Her doll!

They helped her build a castle . . .

then launched a sneak attack.

They gave her hugs and kisses,

dropping ice cubes down her back.

They ate up all the chocolate pie
and polished off the cream.

They crept up on her
in the dark to see if
she would . . .

They dug worms with her violin,
went fishing with her bow.

They let her be the bad guy . . .

. . . and forgot to let her go.

Anna had a dozen cousins.
None of them were girls.

And Anna, if you asked her,
wouldn't trade them for the world.